Phonics Friends

Olivia by the Ocean
The Sound of Long O

The Child's World

By Cecilia Minden and Joanne Meier

The Child's World

Published in the United States of America
by The Child's World®
PO Box 326
Chanhassen, MN 55317-0326
800-599-READ
www.childsworld.com

The Child's World®: Mary Berendes, Publishing Director

Editorial Directions, Inc.: E. Russell Primm, Editorial Director
and Project Editor; Katie Marsico, Associate Editor; Judith
Shiffer, Associate Editor and School Media Specialist;
Linda S. Koutris, Photo Researcher and Selector

The Design Lab: Kathleen Petelinsek, Design and Page
Production

Photographs ©: Corbis/Peter Johnson: 6; Getty Images/
Botanica/Mealanie Acevedo: 8; Getty Images/The Image
Bank/Ghislain and Marie David de Lossy: cover, 20;
Images/The Image Bank/G. K. and Vikki Hart: 10; Getty
Images/Photodisc Green: 16; Getty Images/Photodisc
Green/Rob Melnychuk: 14; Getty Getty Images/Stone/
Bob Thomas: 12; Getty Images/Taxi: 4; Getty Images/
Taxi/Adrian Lyon: 18.

Library of Congress Cataloging-in-Publication Data
Minden, Cecilia.
  Olivia by the ocean : the sound of long O / by Cecilia
Minden and Joanne Meier.
    p. cm. — (Phonics friends)
  Summary: Simple text featuring the long "o" sound
describes Olivia's walk by the ocean.
  ISBN 1-59296-320-X (library bound : alk. paper)
[1. English language—Phonetics. 2. Reading.] I. Meier,
Joanne D. II. Title. III. Series.
  PZ7.M6539Ol 2004
  [E]—dc22   2004002234

Note to parents and educators:

The Child's World® has created Phonics Friends with the goal of exposing children to engaging stories and pictures that assist in phonics development. The books in the series will help children learn the relationships between the letters of written language and the individual sounds of spoken language. This contact helps children learn to use these relationships to read and write words.

The books in this series follow a similar format. An introductory page, to be read by an adult, introduces the child to the phonics feature, or sound, that will be highlighted in the book. Read this page to the child, stressing the phonic feature. Help the student learn how to form the sound with her mouth. The Phonics Friends story and engaging photographs follow the introduction. At the end of the story, word lists categorize the feature words into their phonic element. Additional information on using these lists is on The Child's World® Web site listed at the top of this page.

Each book in this series has been carefully written to meet specific readability requirements. Close attention has been paid to elements such as word count, sentence length, and vocabulary. Readability formulas measure the ease with which the text can be read and understood. Each Phonics Friends book has been analyzed using the Spache readability formula. For more information on this formula, as well as the levels for each of the books in this series please visit The Child's World® Web site.

Reading research suggests that systematic phonics instruction can greatly improve students' word recognition, spelling, and comprehension skills. The Phonics Friends series assists in the teaching of phonics by providing students with important opportunities to apply their knowledge of phonics as they read words, sentences, and text.

The letter *o* makes two sounds.

The short sound of *o* sounds like *o* as in:

    job and *box.*

The long sound of *o* sounds like *o* as in:

    open and *rope.*

In this book, you will read words that have the long *o* sound as in:

    ocean, stone, toes, and *home.*

Olivia lives by the ocean.

She is going to walk by

the water.

She finds some stones.

Those stones are so pretty!

She pokes her toes in the sand.

Oh, the sand feels good.

Olivia walks over to a little puppy.

"Are you all alone, little puppy?"

She pets the puppy's soft nose.

Here comes Olivia's friend, Toby.

"You found my puppy, Pokey," says Toby.

"I left the door open.

Pokey ran out. Thank you

for finding him," says Toby.

"I also have a puppy. Her name is Opal," says Olivia.

It is time for Olivia to go home.

Olivia waves to Toby and Pokey.

"I hope I see you tomorrow!"

Fun Facts

The Pacific Ocean is the world's largest ocean, and it is also the deepest. This ocean touches four continents—North America, South America, Asia, and Australia. Other major oceans are the Atlantic, Indian, and Arctic. Unlike the freshwater in most lakes and rivers, the water in oceans contains salt. Some plants and animals are able to live only in freshwater, while others such as sharks and whales are able to live only in saltwater.

If your parents own a toolbox, you might notice that most of the tools are made of metal. But people didn't always work with metal tools. Two to five million years ago, they used tools made of bone, wood, and stone. For this reason, that period of time became known as the Stone Age.

Activity

Learning about Your Birthstone

Every month has a precious stone, or gem, that is known as a birthstone. If you were born in January, your birthstone is a red stone known as a garnet. The birthstone for April is a diamond. If you were born in September, your birthstone is a blue stone known as a sapphire. Find out what your birthstone is!

To Learn More

Books
About the Sound of Long O
Klingel, Cynthia, and Robert B. Noyed. *On My Boat: The Sound of Long O.* Chanhassen, Minn.: The Child's World, 2000.

About Oceans
Berger, Melvin, and Gilda Berger. *What Makes an Ocean Wave?: Questions and Answers about Ocean Life.* New York: Scholastic, 2001.
Cole, Joanna, and Bruce Degen (illustrator). *The Magic School Bus on the Ocean Floor.* New York: Scholastic, 1992.

About Stones
Muth, Jon J. *Stone Soup.* New York: Scholastic, 2003.
Pfister, Marcus, and Marianne Martens (translator). *Milo and the Magical Stones.* New York: North-South Books, 1997.
Trimble, Marcia, and Susi Grell (illustrator). *Malinda Martha and Her Stepping Stones.* Los Altos Hills, Calif.: Images Press, 1999.

Web Sites
Visit our home page for lots of links about the Sound of Long O:

http://www.childsworld.com/links.html

Note to Parents, Teachers, and Librarians: We routinely check our Web links to make sure they're safe, active sites—so encourage your readers to check them out!

Long O
Feature Words

Proper Names

Olivia

Opal

Pokey

Toby

Feature Words in Initial Position

ocean

oh

open

over

Feature Words with Consonant-Vowel-Silent E Pattern

alone

home

hope

nose

poke

stone

Feature Words with Other Vowel Patterns

go

going

so

toe

About the Authors

Cecilia Minden, PhD, directs the Language and Literacy Program at the Harvard Graduate School of Education. She is a reading specialist with classroom and administrative experience in grades K–12. She earned her PhD in reading education from the University of Virginia. Cecilia and her husband Dave Cupp enjoy sharing their love of reading with their granddaughter Chelsea.

Joanne Meier, PhD, has worked as an elementary school teacher and university professor. She earned her BA in early childhood education from the University of South Carolina, and her MEd and PhD in education from the University of Virginia. She currently works as a literacy consultant for schools and private organizations. Joanne Meier lives with her husband Eric, and spends most of her time chasing her two daughters, Kella and Erin, and her two cats, Sam and Gilly, in Charlottesville, Virginia.